10/17

TAKE
TED
INSTEAD

For Jazzy, Ryder and Aurora. CW

For Patrick. AF

First American Edition 2017
Kane Miller, A Division of EDC Publishing

Text copyright © 2016 Cassandra Webb
Illustrations copyright © 2016 Amanda Francey

First published in Australia in 2016 by New Frontier Publishing Pty Ltd
Translation rights arranged through Australian Licensing Corporation

For information contact:
Kane Miller, A Division of EDC Publishing
P.O. Box 470663
Tulsa, OK 74147-0663

www.kanemiller.com
www.edcpub.com
www.usbornebooksandmore.com

Library of Congress Control Number: 2016955641

Printed and bound in China
1 2 3 4 5 6 7 8 9 10

ISBN: 978-1-61067-618-2

TAKE TED INSTEAD

Cassandra Webb ★ Illustrated by Amanda Francey

Kane Miller
A DIVISION OF EDC PUBLISHING

It's time for bed, sleepyhead.

No, no, take **RED** instead.

It's time for bed, sleepyhead.

No, no, take **SEB** instead.

It's time for bed, sleepyhead.

No, no, take **FRED** instead.

It's time for bed, sleepyhead.

No, no, take **JEDD** instead.

It's time for bed, sleepyhead.

No, no, take **ZED** instead.

It's time for bed, sleepyhead.

No, no, take
NED
instead.

It's time for bed, sleepyhead.

No, no, take **ED** instead.

It's time for bed,
sleepyhead.

No, no, take **TED** instead.

But Ted will be lonely,
in bed all on his own.

Take **ME** too.